Bad Dog

and

No, Nell, No!

'Bad Dog' and 'No, Nell, No!'
An original concept by Elizabeth Dale
© Elizabeth Dale

Illustrated by Julia Seal

Published by MAVERICK ARTS PUBLISHING LTD

Studio 3A, City Business Centre, 6 Brighton Road,

Horsham, West Sussex, RH13 5BB

© Maverick Arts Publishing Limited July 2017

+44 (0)1403 256941

A CIP catalogue record for this book is available at the British Library.

ISBN 978-1-84886-287-6

arts publishing
www.maverickbooks.co.uk

This book is rated as: Pink Band (Guided Reading)
This story is decodable at Letters and Sounds Phase 2.

Bad Dog

and

No, Nell, No!

By
Elizabeth Dale

Illustrated by
Julia Seal

The Letter D

Trace the lower and upper case letter with a finger. Sound out the letter.

Around,
up,
down

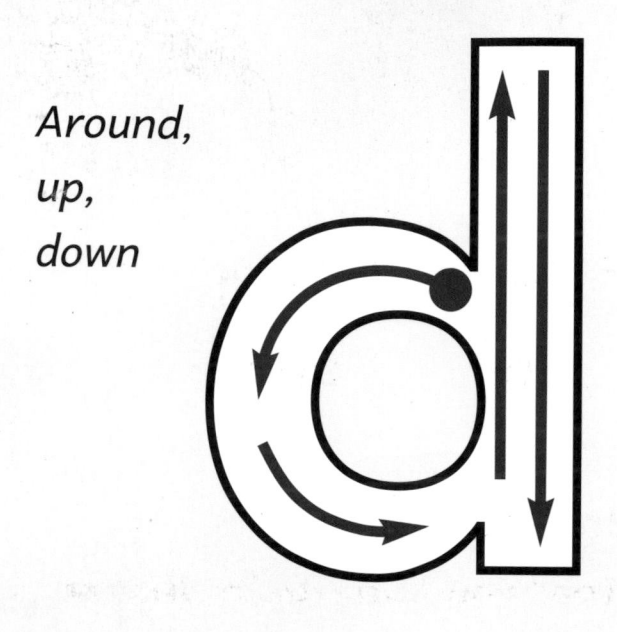

Down,
up,
around

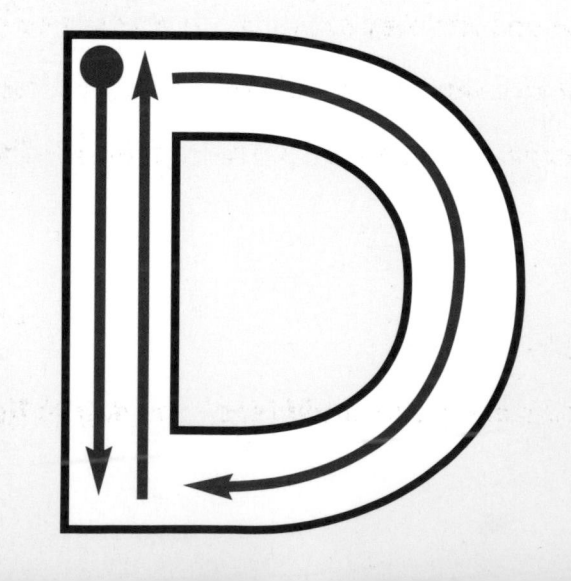

Some words to familiarise:

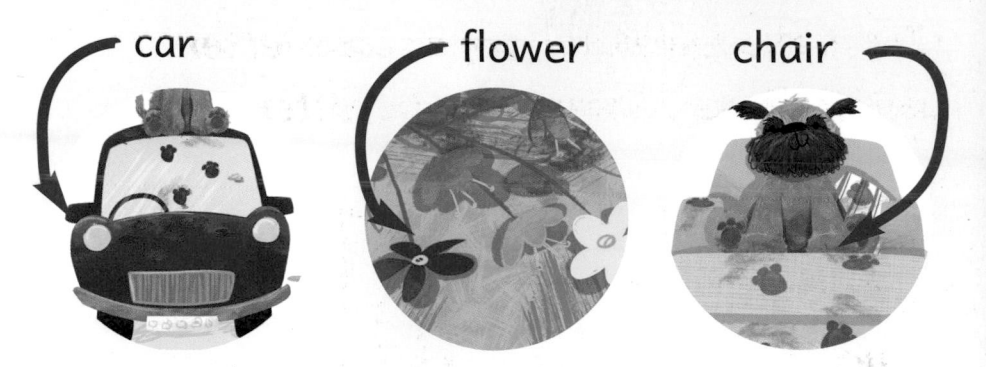

car   flower   chair

High-frequency words:

the   on   dad

Tips for Reading 'Bad Dog'

- Practise the words listed above before reading the story.

- If the reader struggles with any of the other words, ask them to look for sounds they know in the word. Encourage them to sound out the words and help them read the words if necessary.

- After reading the story, ask the reader what the dog was doing.

Fun Activity

Discuss how everyone could teach the dog to be better behaved.

Bad Dog

The bad dog sits on the car.

The bad dog sits on the flowers.

The bad dog sits on the rug.

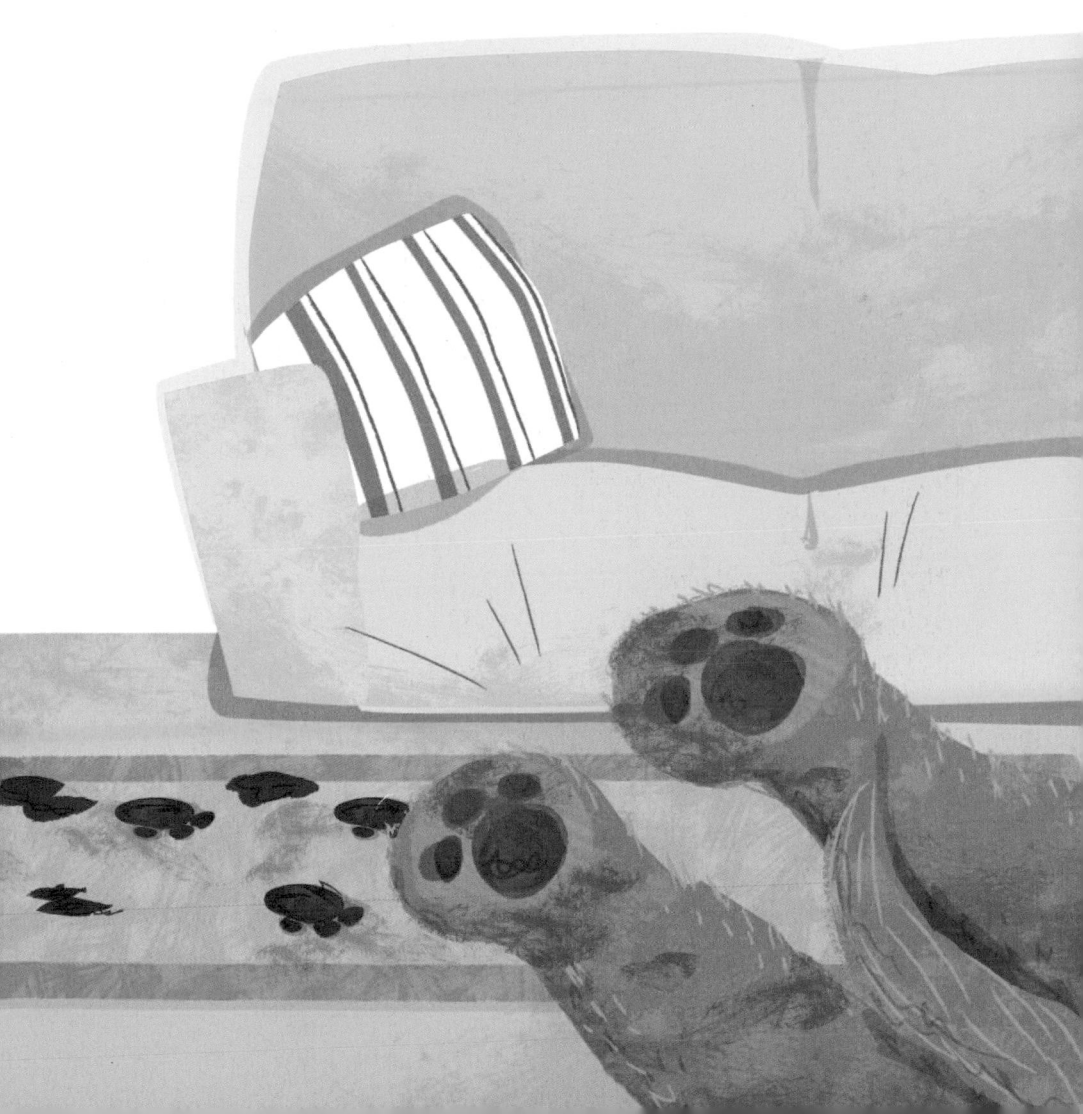

The bad dog sits on the chair.

The bad dog sits on Dad!

The Letter N

Trace the lower and upper case letter with a finger. Sound out the letter.

Down,
up,
around,
down

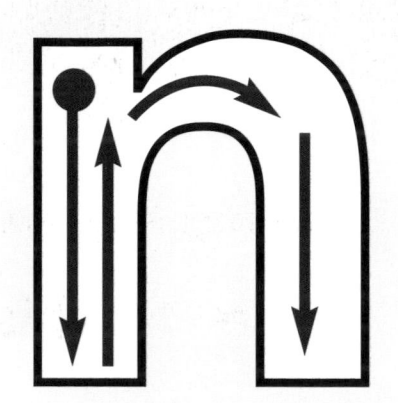

Down,
up,
down,
up

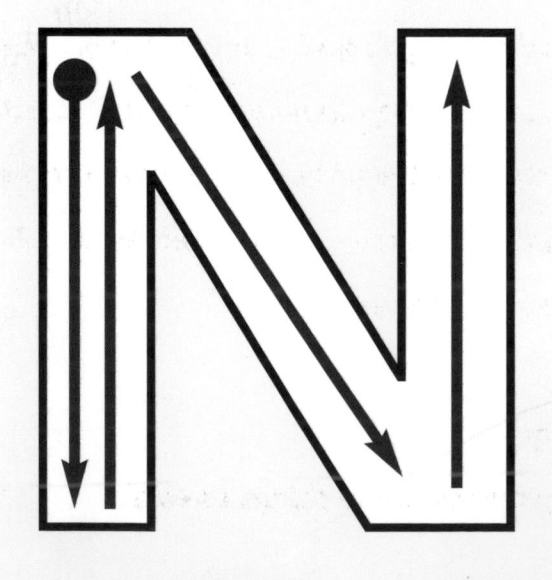

Some words to familiarise:

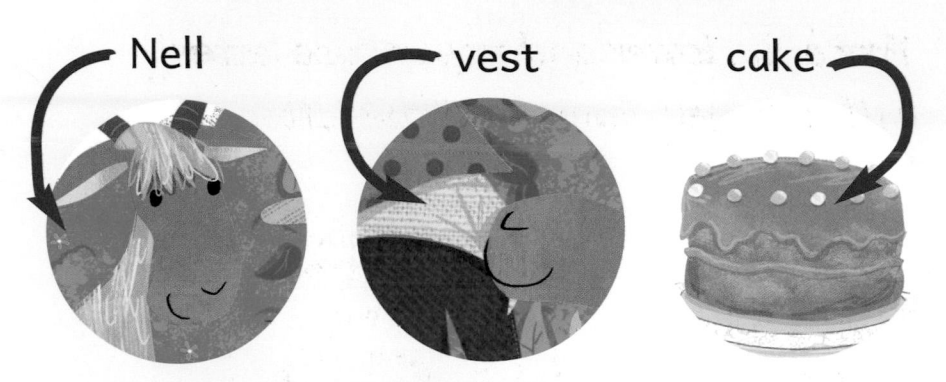

Nell   vest   cake

High-frequency words:

no   this

Tips for Reading 'No, Nell, No!'

- Practise the words listed above before reading the story.

- If the reader struggles with any of the other words, ask them to look for sounds they know in the word. Encourage them to sound out the words and help them read the words if necessary.

- After reading the story, ask the reader why Nell did not want to eat her dinner at the end.

Fun Activity

What are your favourite things to eat?

No, Nell, No!

Nell eats this bag.

Nell eats this sock.

Nell eats this vest.

Nell eats this hat.

Nell eats this cake.

Book Bands for Guided Reading

The Institute of Education book banding system is a scale of colours that reflects the various levels of reading difficulty. The bands are assigned by taking into account the content, the language style, the layout and phonics.

Maverick Early Readers are a bright, attractive range of books covering the pink to purple bands. All of these books have been book banded for guided reading to the industry standard and edited by a leading educational consultant.

For more titles visit:
www.maverickbooks.co.uk/early-readers

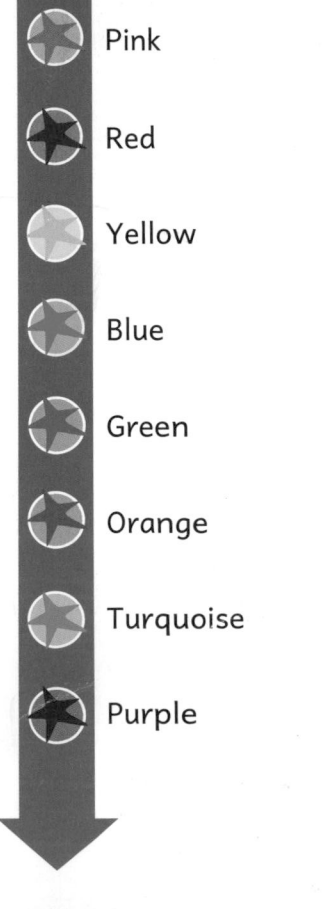

Pink

Red

Yellow

Blue

Green

Orange

Turquoise

Purple

Book Band

Pink

Bad Dog and No, Nell, No!	978-1-84886-287-6
Meg and Rat and Puff! Puff! Puff!	978-1-84886-286-9
Ned in Bed and Fun at the Park	978-1-84886-285-2
Cool Duck and Lots of Hats	978-1-84886-249-4
Peck, Hen, Peck! and Ben's Pet	978-1-84886-248-7